Bashful

Saddle Up Series
Book 1

Dave and Pat Sargent are longtime residents of Prairie Grove, Arkansas. Dave, a fourth-generation dairy farmer, began writing in early December 1990. Pat, a former teacher, began writing in the fourth grade. They enjoy the outdoors and have a real love for animals.

Bashful

Saddle Up Series
Book 1

By Dave and Pat Sargent

Beyond "The End"
By Sue Rogers

Illustrated by Jane Lenoir

Ozark Publishing, Inc.
P.O. Box 228
Prairie Grove, AR 72753

Cataloging-in-Publication Data

Sargent, Dave, 1941—
    Bashful / by Dave and Pat Sargent ;
illustrated by Jane Lenoir.—Prairie Grove, AR :
Ozark Publishing, c2004.
    p. cm. (Saddle up series ; 1)

    "Be brave"—Cover.
    SUMMARY: Bashful is a dun-colored
horse who helps his master explore the
Great Salt Lake in Utah. Includes factual
information about dusty dun horses.
    ISBN 1-56763-683-7 (hc)
          1-56763-684-5 (pbk)

    1. Horses—Juvenile fiction. [1. Horses—
Fiction. 2. Utah—Fiction.] I. Sargent, Pat, 1936–
II. Lenoir, Jane, 1950– ill. III. Title. IV. Series.

    PZ10.3.S24Bas 2004
    [Fic]—dc21   2001005631

Printed in the United States of America

Inspired by

dusty dun horses we've seen along the highways and byways.

Dedicated to

all kids who love bashful people and bashful pets. Have you ever seen your dog or cat, or even your horse, blush?

Foreword

Bashful is a bashful dusty dun. His boss, Jim Bridger, is a famous expedition leader, Indian fighter, and trapper. Together, they discover the Great Salt Lake in Utah Territory.

Contents

If you would like to have the authors of the Saddle Up Series visit your school, free of charge, call 1-800-321-5671 or 1-800-960-3876.

One

Jim Bridger Needs a Horse

The sun was peeking over the eastern horizon when the cowboys of the Rocking S Horse Ranch entered the corral. For three or four minutes, they stood, watching the horses move nervously around them. "Hmmm," Bashful the dusty dun thought. "This is highly unusual. Normally they would have already roped the mounts that they were going to ride for the day."

"What are they doing?" the strawberry roan nickered.

"I don't know," the flea-bitten grey replied. "But I don't like the way they are acting."

Bashful quietly walked up between them and whispered, "Just stay calm. Maybe something good is about to happen."

"Yeah, right!" the black horse snorted.

The ranch foreman and a tall man with a dark beard walked to the corral fence.

"Have you boys found the right horse for Mr. James Bridger yet?" he asked with a chuckle.

"Whew," Bashful snorted. "If that's their problem, I can help."

He slowly approached the tall man with his ears pointed forward. Mr. Bridger reached out and patted him gently on the neck.

"You would make a fine boss," Bashful whinnied as he nuzzled the man's hand with his upper lip.

Jim Bridger smiled. "You can stop looking, men. I like the looks and disposition of this dusty dun."

The ranch foreman nodded his head and replied, "Bashful is a level-headed horse, Jim. He has a lot of grit, so I think the two of you would make a pretty good team."

Jim's eyes sparkled with good humor as he said, "That's real good. I need a good partner to trap beavers, trade furs, fight Indians, and help guide expeditions through the wild frontier."

"Wow! You are one busy boss," Bashful nickered. "Did you hear that, my good horse friends? Life with a boss like Jim Bridger is going to be exciting!"

"And a lot of hard work," the appaloosa grumbled.

One hour later, Bashful was brushed and saddled. As Jim slid his left boot into the stirrup, Bashful smiled real big. "Hmmm," he thought. "My life is taking a sudden turn into adventure. I like that!"

After traveling at a slow pace for days, Bashful and his new boss stopped early one evening. While setting up camp beside a stream, Jim built a fire as the dusty dun grazed nearby. During the supper meal, Jim spoke of his early years.

"Bashful," he said between bites of food, "I was born March 17, 1804, in Richmond, Virginia. But," he added with a chuckle, "I guess my ole daddy didn't like being an innkeeper or a surveyor, because we moved to a farm in Illinois eight years later."

"That doesn't sound exciting," Bashful murmured.

Jim leaned back against a tree stump and yawned.

"I was bored with life on the farm," he said sleepily. "I wanted excitement and adventure."

Seconds later, Bashful smiled and yawned as gentle snores from his boss echoed amid the sounds of night.

"Boss," he murmured quietly, "the longer I'm around you, the more I like and respect you. I am one lucky dusty dun."

Three hours later, Bashful heard a strange noise. He nuzzled Jim's whiskers and whinnied softly.

Jim Bridger opened one eye and mumbled, "Go back to sleep, Bashful. It's too early to get up."

Again, the dusty dun heard a noise. It was footsteps, he decided, then nudged Jim in his ribs. This time Jim sat up and growled, "Well, what do you want now?"

"I want your help," a voice responded from among the trees.

Jim leaped to his feet with his rifle in his hand. Bashful scooted backward, then muttered, "That's what I wanted to talk to you about, Boss. We just may be in a heap of danger."

Two

Pioneer Family Lost

Bashful and Jim remained tense and watchful as they listened for an explanation from their unexpected visitor.

"Don't shoot," a man's voice said. "I'm not here to do you harm. My family and I are trying to go west to start a new life in the wild frontier. We've been lost for five days now."

"Come closer," Jim ordered. "If you're telling the truth, maybe we can help you."

As the stranger approached, Bashful noticed that he was a young, clean-shaven man who was nervous.

"I saw your campfire," he said hoarsely, "and figured you may know this territory. My wife and two youngsters are waiting for me about a mile from here."

"Sit down," Jim said. "I'll get you a cup of coffee while you tell me where you're wanting to go."

As the two men talked, Bashful sighed, "Whew, I'm sure glad he isn't a wild Indian or a grouchy bear. I'm not ready for that yet."

Two hours later, the dawn of a new day illuminated the lone wagon and team of horses in the distance. Bashful neighed a loud greeting as he and the two men approached. Then his ears flattened against his head as he saw a rifle barrel sticking out of the covered wagon. It was pointed straight at him.

"Mercy," he groaned. "I should have kept my neigh to myself."

"Don't shoot, Molly! It's me!" the young pioneer yelled. "I've found help. Jim Bridger is going to show us the way to our new home site."

As the gun barrel was replaced by the faces of a young woman and two little children, Bashful breathed a sigh of relief. Hearing a chuckle from the team, he looked at the bay sabino.

"What's so funny?" he growled.

"Boss Lady does not know how to shoot a gun," the bay snickered.

"She would probably shoot herself in the foot," the chestnut sabino added with a loud chuckle.

Bashful glared at the two horses and growled, "That wouldn't stop her from accidentally shooting me."

"No," they agreed. "It sure wouldn't. We're real sorry for your scary introduction to the Updike family. They're really nice folks."

Two weeks later, Bashful and his Jim Bridger boss led the little family into a fertile valley in Utah Territory.

"Stop, Jim Bridger!" came a sudden yell from Mr. Updike. "This looks like home to us." He pointed to a stream of water and a big grove of trees. "There's plenty of water, and I'll build our home out of some of the trees."

Bashful and Jim smiled and nodded.

"They will have a good happy life here," Jim Bridger said quietly. "It's time for you and me to explore some new country, Bashful."

"I'm ready, willing, and able, Boss," Bashful neighed loudly. "Let's go!"

Two nights later, the dusty dun and the tall bearded trapper were again setting up camp by themselves.

"Where shall we go from here, Bashful?" Jim asked. "There's a whole wide frontier out there that we can explore."

While pawing the ground with one front hoof, the dusty dun nodded his head.

"Shall we go south or north or west, partner?" the trapper inquired.

"Hmmm," Bashful murmured. "It sounds like any direction is going to be exciting." He whirled to the left and set his hoof down, firmly pointing it in a definite direction.

Jim laughed and said, "Okay, Bashful. We go northwest in the morning. You better get some sleep because I don't know what we may meet up with out there."

The dusty dun shook his head and snorted, "Whatever we come across, Boss, won't matter. We can handle it."

Three

The Great Salt Lake

For several days, Bashful and Jim Bridger wandered through the fascinating and beautiful Utah Territory. Slowly traveling northwest, they enjoyed colorful sunrises, enchanting scenery, and beautiful sunsets. They met and visited with two separate caravans of pioneers who were traveling west in covered wagons.

"Hello there! Where are you going?" Bashful asked a pretty sorrel mare.

She actually winked at Bashful before replying, "My boss said we are going to California. If you travel that far west, stop and see me."

The dusty dun felt the skin beneath his coat grow warmer, and he looked away.

"Thanks," he murmured, "but Boss and I are going a different direction."

Suddenly he heard Jim calling his name. "Whee. Thank goodness," he thought. "I'm beginning to feel mighty uncomfortable with this little sorrel gal."

"I'm on my way, Boss," he quickly neighed. "Good-bye and good luck in California," he added as he trotted toward Jim.

"Let's get away from here, Boss," he muttered. "I seem to get along better with rocks and trees and mountains and sand."

One afternoon a few days later, Jim suddenly pointed ahead.

"Look at that mirage, Bashful," he said. "It looks like a huge lake of water, but it isn't really there."

"Huh?" Bashful whinnied. "What do you mean by that, Boss? It's there. I can see it."

Jim laughed and said, "Heat waves drift upward and play tricks with your vision. It makes you think that you're seeing something that isn't really there. This fake picture is called a mirage."

"But I know it's there, Boss," Bashful nickered as he quickened his pace into a slow lope. "I'll prove it to you."

A short time later, the dusty dun skidded to a halt on the shore of a huge clear blue lake.

"Wow!" Jim said quietly. "I have never seen such a beautiful body of water in all of my life."

He swung his right leg over the back of the saddle and stepped

down. A moment later, he dipped
his hand into the lake for a drink.

Meanwhile, Bashful hurried to the water's edge.

"It looks cold and refreshing," he muttered as he dipped his nose in.

"Yuk!" both horse and rider sputtered. "That is terrible stuff!"

As the dusty dun pawed the white granules that were scattered around the edge of the water, Jim chipped off a big white crust from beneath the surface. He carefully put his tongue against it.

"Salt!" he shouted. "This entire lake is full of salt!"

"Hmmm," Bashful muttered thoughtfully. "I guess I should have been paying better attention to our surroundings, Boss. I don't even see a bird or a lizard around here. Their absence would have told me to be more careful."

"This great salt lake may be worthless for drinking water," Jim murmured. "But it is one beautiful and unique sample of Mother Nature at her best."

The sun was below the western horizon when Bashful and his boss bedded down for the night on the barren desert sand. As darkness descended upon the Utah Territory, Jim Bridger looked up at the stars and nodded his head.

"Those twinkling little lights look like we could reach up and touch them, Bashful. They sure are pretty, aren't they?"

"Uh-huh," Bashful nickered. "Now go to sleep, Boss. Maybe we can find some good drinking water if we get started early enough in the morning." He paused when he heard the tall gentle man snoring, and then added, "Good night, Boss."

"Hmmm," Bashful thought as he watched Jim sleep. "One day history books will probably tell the story of Jim Bridger and his feats as an explorer, Indian fighter, trapper, and expedition leader. The pages will describe his discovery of the Great Salt Lake. But I wonder if folks will remember his dusty dun horse."

Suddenly he chuckled and said, "It doesn't matter if folks remember me or not. Life with Jim Bridger is good and fun and interesting. And it just keeps getting better and better!"

Four

Dusty Dun Facts

The term *dun* is often used to describe yellow horses with black points. The term is also used loosely to describe all lighter horse colors, some of which have no black points.

Some cowboys separate the horses that have yellow bodies, black points, and primitive marks and call them duns, thus reserving *buckskin* for those without the marks.

If buckskins or zebra duns have a brownish cast to their yellow coats, they are called dusty duns or dusty buckskins, and they look very much like olive grullos without the dark head.

Dusty Dun

BEYOND "THE END"

*A horseman should know
neither fear nor anger.*
James Rarey

WORD LIST
dusty dun
trap beavers
little and often
flat against head
strawberry roan
flank
fight Indians
hindquarters
flea-bitten grey
never work after meal—wait 1 hour
shot forward
black
dock
guide expeditions

37

bay sabino
trade furs
explore new places
chestnut sabino
twitch back and forth
croup
sorrel

From the word list above, write:

1. Two groups of words that tell impor-
tant things to remember about feeding a
horse.
2. Four words that name points of a
horse.
3. Five words that tell what Jim Bridger
needed a good horse to help him do.
4. Six words that are color names for
horses.
5. Three ear positions for a horse.

Tell what signal a horse is giving for each
position of his ears.

CURRICULUM CONNECTIONS

The ranch foreman told Jim Bridger that Bashful had a lot of grit. What did he mean?

Look up the word *grit* in three different dictionaries. Does *grit* have more than one meaning? Which meaning do you think might describe Bashful and explain what the ranch foreman meant? How many synonyms can you find in the three dictionaries for *grit*?

Do you know someone who has grit? Who? Why do you say that person has grit?

Why is the Great Salt Lake salty? How many tons of dissolved salts enter the lake each year?

Four main rivers flow into the Great Salt

Lake but none flow out! Why does the lake not get bigger and bigger?

See answers and more interesting facts about this lake and ancient Lake Bonneville at <www.geology.utah. gov/online/PI-39/index.htm>. (Be sure to type the capital letters PI exactly as shown.)

Was Jim Bridger a real person?

Was he the first man to discover the Great Salt Lake?

PROJECT

Combine your math and artistic skills! Draw to scale and accurately color a picture (body, tail, and mane) of the horse that is featured in each book read in the Saddle Up Series. You could soon have sixty horses prancing around the walls of your classroom!
Learning + horses = FUN.

Look in your school library media center for books about how to draw a horse and the colors of horses. Don't forget the useful information in the last chapter of this book (Dusty Dun Facts) and the picture on the book cover for a shape and color guide.

HELPFUL HINTS AND WEBSITES
A horse is measured in hands. One hand equals four inches. Use a scale of 1" equals 1 hand.

41

Visit website <www.equisearch.com> to find a glossary of equine terms, information about tack and equipment, breeds, art and graphics, and more about horses. Learn more at <www.horse-country. com> and at <www.ansi.okstate.edu/ breeds/horses/>.

KidsClick! is a web search for kids by librarians. There are many interesting websites here. HORSES and HORSE-MANSHIP are two of the more than 600 subjects. Visit <www.kidsclick.org>.

Is your classroom beginning to look like the Rocking S Horse Ranch? Happy Trails to You!